WAGONS
WEST

VeraLee Wiggins

Illustrated by
Ken Save

BARBOUR
PUBLISHING, INC.
Uhrichsville, Ohio

All Scripture quotations are taken from the Authorized King James Version of the Bible.

Published by Barbour Publishing, Inc.
       P.O. Box 719
       Uhrichsville, Ohio 44683
       http://www.barbourbooks.com

ecpa Member of the
Evangelical Christian
Publishers Association

Printed in the United States of America.

WAGONS
WEST

HE RELAXED IN HIS SADDLE

CHAPTER 1

Day after tomorrow! The wagon train would leave Independence in two more days on May 4, 1859. David Moreland, with his father, mother, and two sisters would finally begin the long, long trail to Oregon.

Although they'd been planning for six months, David had thought it would never happen. But they'd finally sold the farm, and here he was! Thanks, God. I should have known you'd answer my prayers.

He relaxed in his saddle as Thunder, his enormous black gelding, carried him around and through the gathering wagons. Many wagons. David had counted eleven, and more kept rolling in. Every wagon wore a white bonnet. That's what David called the rounded tops because they'd put them on to protect the people from the wet rain and hot sun.

He wished they could have used the famous

Conestoga wagons. The Conestogas were much bigger and heavier, so no one used them on the long Oregon Trail where they had steep mountains to cross. Pa said it was asking too much from the animals even with the lighter wagons.

Wonderful smells drifted to David as women squatted beside small fires cooking the evening meals. His mouth watered as he inhaled the scent of coffee, meat, potatoes and onions frying.

Smoke swirled around him. Oxen bawled—maybe a million at the same time. Some men laughed in the distance and others swore at animals they worked with. Little children laughed and babies cried.

As Thunder, free to go where he chose, made a right turn between two wagons, David saw a boy a little larger than he, jump onto an ox's back. The large animal bawled and gave a quick twist. The boy managed to stay on, and somehow got his feet under him, then jumped to another ox a few feet away.

THE ANIMAL BAWLED

After a quick bawl that made one drop his rear end, the boy was sent rolling to the dusty ground. David almost laughed until the boy got to his feet and kicked the tethered animal hard in the side with his rigid, leather boot. The animal grunted, dropped to the ground, then gathered his feet under him and stood. The boy drew back his heavy boot again.

David slid off Thunder. "Hey! Don't do it. Don't ever do that again!"

The boy looked shocked, then pulled his shoulders back and matched David's glare with one of his own. "Them oxen yours?" he growled.

"Don't you know they have feelings?"

The boy laughed and walked off. After he'd walked about twenty feet he turned back to David. "I dunno why it matters. Don't you know them animals'll all be dead afore we get to Oregon?" He loped off through the wagons.

David turned Thunder back to his family's wagons,

"HEY! DON'T DO IT!"

a little of the excitement gone. He'd heard The Oregon Trail was hard. Would it really kill animals?

The Morelands had bought eight yoke of oxen the day before. Two oxen made a yoke, so they had sixteen oxen altogether. It took three yokes to pull each wagon, but Pa had bought a few extra, so the animals could rest once in a while. David had wanted mules, but a mule cost $100, an ox only $25. As David thought about all the things before him, Thunder brought him to his own wagons.

"Come and eat, Son," Mrs. Moreland called.

David took off Thunder's bridle and put on a halter, so the large horse could graze without a bit in his mouth. "Get your plate," Mama said. David's sisters, Katie and Annie, already had their plates ready for the steaming food.

After Pa prayed, they sat on wooden boxes and talked while they ate. "Know what we're doin' tomorrow?" Pa asked. "We're gettin' everythin' we need for

"COME AND EAT, SON"

the long trip. Then we'll pack the wagons."

Papa and Mama had brought featherbeds from home, one for their wagon and one for the girls'. David planned to wrap up in a blanket and sleep on the ground.

Right after breakfast the next morning, the Moreland family walked into a general store in Independence, Missouri. They'd planned to buy enough food and supplies for their 2000 mile trip, a journey that would last five months, maybe longer.

"Are you sure the Oregon Trail is safe, Papa?" Annie asked.

"I'm not sure of anything," Papa said, "except everyone's getting two pairs of walking shoes."

David grinned. "I'm not walking much, Pa. Better get the shoes for Thunder."

Besides shoes, they bought four barrels of flour, one barrel of dried beans, lots of green coffee beans, dried peas, bacon, side meat, sugar, salt, and baking powder.

"ARE YOU SURE THE OREGON TRAIL IS SAFE, PAPA?"

A Dutch oven, a large mixing bowl, some cheap pots, dishes, and silver completed the things needed to keep their stomachs happy.

They also bought material, muslin for sheeting and dresses, linsey wool for dresses and shirts, jean for men's clothing, all to make up when they reached Oregon.

David felt like flying all the way back to their wagons. The things they bought had made the adventure ahead seem real.

When they had packed everything into the wagons, Pa got a screwdriver. "Come on, Davy," he said. "We got one more job to do."

David couldn't imagine what was left, but he climbed into the wagon with Pa. Pa got down on his knees and started undoing some screws in the floor. Pretty soon he lifted one of the long floor boards from the wagon and shoved a money pouch beneath the board.

"That there's our grubstake for Oregon," he said

"THAT THERE'S OUR GRUBSTAKE FOR OREGON"

proudly. He winked at David. "This here'll be our little secret, Son."

As David hurried back to the campfire to Mama and the girls, he felt ten feet tall. He and Pa were the men in this family.

But as he lay waiting for sleep to come, he worried just a little about the Oregon Trail. Would it really be all he hoped for? Or would it be too much? Was he man enough for this big thing ahead? *Go with me, God. I'm almost getting scared.*

GO WITH ME, GOD

THE FIRST WAGON MOVED

CHAPTER 2

The sound of cattle bawling, horses whinnying, people yelling, and the smell of food cooking wakened David early the next morning, almost before the sun rose.

This was the day they'd start to Oregon! Jumping out of bed, he threw his clothes on.

He swallowed the fried potatoes and bacon almost without chewing them, and gulped down the bitter coffee. He hadn't been allowed coffee before, so he had to like it, no matter how much it seemed he didn't.

Oxen bawled and mules brayed even louder when the men harnessed and yoked them, then hooked them to the wagons.

The wagon train captain checked all eighteen wagons, making sure everyone was ready. Then he walked to the front wagon and signalled to start!

The first wagon moved. Then, the second. Pretty soon, the long train moved slowly across the prairie.

WAGONS WEST

David guided Thunder away from the train so he could see all the wagons in a row. What a sight! Oxen and mules leaning into their harnesses, one white bonnet after another with hordes of people walking beside them. Loose cattle followed, herded by men on horses.

"Aintcha never seen covered wagons afore?" a nasty voice asked.

David whirled in his saddle to face the boy who'd jumped on the oxen. He rode a small brown and white spotted horse. A harsh answer formed in David's throat but it didn't come out. *A soft answer turneth away wrath* popped into his mind, and he remembered reading the words in the Bible.

He managed a friendly smile. "No, I guess I haven't," he said. "I've heard about them and saw them gathering, but this is the first time I've seen them moving." His eyes returned to the long line of wagons moving slowly west, their tops glistening white against the blue

"AINTCHA NEVER SEEN COVERED WAGONS AFORE?"

sky. "Isn't it—isn't it—magnificent?" he asked.

The other boy glanced toward the wagons. "Don't look like nuthin' special to me. Just a bunch of dumb cows and people crawlin' along the ground."

"Hey," David said, "I'm David Moreland. You got a name?"

"Yeah. Jake Case. What's it to ya?"

His crude answer disappointed David. Touching Thunder's sides with his heels, he turned back toward the wagon train. Jake followed on his pony. About halfway back, David decided to try once more to be Jake's friend. They might be the only boys their age on the whole train. When he gently pulled the slack from Thunder's reins, the big horse stopped. Jake jerked his pony to a stop too.

"I just wondered," David said. "Maybe we could ride together and do things."

Jake looked bored. "Whadda you do?"

"I race my horse, I can run, and I can throw a rock.

"I'M DAVID MORELAND"

Do you like baseball? Pa let me bring my ball and bat.'

Jake snorted. "I figgered you wasn't nuthin but a baby." Without warning, he gave Thunder a hard kick on the rear end, dug his heels into his pony, and took off.

After calming himself, then Thunder, David rode back to the wagon train. He'd for sure leave that mean boy alone now.

"How you doing, Son?" Mama asked as he reined Thunder to a walk beside her and Katie. Annie drove the oxen.

"Good. I rode off so I could see the wagon train. It looks good, Ma."

She nodded absently, walking briskly through the grass beside the wagon. "Better stick around, Davy. We'll be nooning soon, and I'll need something to make a fire."

When the wagons stopped for nooning—the noon rest, and food and water for people and animals—David found plenty of dry sticks from bushes and large weeds.

"I FIGGERED YOU WASN'T NOTHIN BUT A BABY"

Ma mixed up some biscuits from flour, baking powder, salt, and water. Then she put them into the thing she called a Dutch oven and put it on the fire. She smiled at her three children, who watched intently. "That's a little oven that goes over the fire so we can bake food on our long journey."

She fried potatoes and bacon again. "The potatoes won't keep long," she explained, "but we'll enjoy them for a few days."

In about an hour and a half, the captain got everyone moving again.

Pa drove the oxen on one wagon. Mama, Annie, and David would take turns driving the other. Annie had taken first turn with their wagon, and now Mama drove. David couldn't wait for his turn. "Can I drive your oxen, Pa?" David asked. Pa gladly let him walk beside the working animals, encouraging them onward, leading them around holes, big weeds, or whatever got in the way.

"THE POTATOES WON'T KEEP LONG"

After an hour or so, Pa took over the oxen, so David climbed back onto Thunder's tall back.

When David took his turn driving oxen, Annie or Katie rode the big horse.

When they stopped for the night, the captain, Joseph Penberry, showed the drivers how to "corral" the wagons. After the first wagon stopped, each wagon pulled up with the front wheels beside the back wheels of the one in front. The wagon's back wheels turned several feet left. In this way they formed a circle. The teams all ended up inside the circle but were soon unyoked or unharnessed and led outside for water and grass.

The corralled wagons made a barricade of great strength in which to keep the stock during the night and resist Indian attacks. They built the camp fires inside and set up the tents in there, too.

Penberry came around later that evening and gave Pa a little book. "It's the Mormon guide book, the best

"IT'S THE MORMON GUIDE BOOK"

around," he told Pa. "It tells all about The Trail. Better hang onto it."

Pa got close to the fire and read parts of the guide book. "It tells how far important places are from Independence," he told his family, "and where we're likely to find Indians. This is pretty good." When bedtime came, Mama, Pa, Annie, David and Katie all read their Bibles together around the campfire. Then Pa asked God to be with them, to keep them safe and to be sure they all remembered Him.

When they finished, David pulled his blanket from his parents' wagon, lay down by the fire and rolled up in his blanket. Lying there alone, looking up at the millions of stars twinkling in the black sky, he felt a little lonely even though his family slept nearby.

He'd barely fallen asleep when a slight noise awakened him. Someone slunk through the grass toward him! He came wide awake but couldn't get his terrified mouth open to call for help.

PA ASKED GOD TO BE WITH THEM

As he watched the person bumble toward him, he shrank into his blanket, holding perfectly still. Maybe the man wouldn't see him in the dark.

But the figure headed straight at him. David didn't see any feathers, but the man could still be an Indian. He could have left his feathers at home.

David felt helpless lying on the ground all wrapped up. Finally, he came off the ground with a huge leap and faced the man who seemed a little taller and heavier than he.

The man jumped back and David held his ground. Then he slowly advanced toward the man, standing tall, hoping to bluff the man into leaving.

"Whatcha think yer doin'?" a gruff voice whispered.

Jake! What did Jake think he was doing? David felt more frightened now than when it could have been an Indian.

DAVID HELD HIS GROUND

"WHAT DO YOU WANT?"

CHAPTER 3

David considered yelling for Pa but changed his mind. "What do you want?" he asked Jake.

"I seen you sleeping alone over here alone and knew you'd be scared clean outta yer skin. If'n you promise to be quiet, I'll sleep here too, so's you won't go waking up everone." He threw down a blanket about five feet from David's and crawled in. So did David. Neither said anything. David watched, almost certain Jake hadn't come out of the goodness of his heart.

After awhile, David began to feel sleepy but feared to fall asleep with Jake so near. Pretty soon he could hardly hold his eyes open. *Be with me God, while I sleep.*

But almost before he got the words out Jake climbed out of his blanket. David barely breathed, watching him in the dark. Jake picked up his blanket, moved it to about three feet from David's, and crawled back in.

Why would Jake do that? He must be up to something. David decided not to sleep at all.

The next thing David knew, the sun shown in his eyes and morning sounds and smells filled the air. Cattle bawling, babies crying, Mama calling. He'd better get up.

Then he saw Jake, his blanket so close it overlapped David's. David piled out of bed and put on his shoes. "Get up, Jake," he said.

Jake jumped to his feet. "Whadda you want?" he growled.

Mama appeared. "Breakfast is nearly ready," she said. "You boys run down to the creek and wash your hands and faces."

Jake studied her face.

"Yes," she said smiling. "We want you to eat with us. David will you introduce your friend?"

David almost told her Jake wasn't his friend, but introduced him instead.

"YES...WE WANT YOU TO EAT WITH US"

WAGONS WEST

Pa asked God's blessing on the food and the day's journey. Mama dipped bacon and potatoes into all the dishes, dropped buttered biscuits on top, and gave everyone coffee.

Pa learned Jake's name, then asked about his family. "Ain't got none but Pa," Jake answered. "Ma died two years ago. Pa don't care where I am, long's I stay outta his way."

Mama marched over to Jake and hugged him. "You can hang around here. I love you already."

Jake twisted away looking embarrassed. He didn't say much more during breakfast, but David noticed him watching Annie. "Gotta git," Jake said when he finished his breakfast. He didn't say "thank you," or even "good-bye."

Soon the wagon train moved again. They forded a river that day. The men hooked six yokes of oxen to each wagon, then waded through the river beside the oxen to keep them going. The oxen didn't like the cold

"PA DON'T CARE WHERE I AM"

swift water and tried to turn back many times, but the men used their whips until the animals waded through. The crossing took all day.

Jake didn't appear again until night, when he slunk over with his blanket and dropped it to the ground, touching David's again.

"How old're you?" David asked.

"Fourteen. What're you, twelve?"

David laughed happily, losing his last fear of Jake. "I'm fifteen and three months," he said.

Later it began raining. David woke up, wondering what to do. Then he noticed the wagons. "Wake up, Jake," he whispered. "We have to crawl under the wagon." Jake sleepily followed David to the wagon, shoved his blanket under and crawled in.

David slept so hard, he didn't notice water running under the wagon. The next morning he jumped up cold and soaked. It rained so hard Mama couldn't start a fire, so she handed everyone hard cold biscuits, and not

"WHAT'RE YOU...TWELVE?"

enough to fill a boy's stomach.

About two hours later, the train came to a narrow stream so swollen by the rain, it was too deep and swift to ford. The men cut trees bordering the river with their long saws, a man on each end. Then they hauled the heavy logs to the most shallow spot and made a nearly stable bridge. As the group ate dinner, they rejoiced getting safely across.

After nooning, David spotted Jake riding his spotted pony off to one side. He leaned forward, touched Thunder with his toes, and soon reached Jake who didn't welcome him.

"Ya gotta follow me everplace I go?" he growled, shivering as the unrelenting rain continued.

"Want to race?" David asked.

Jake sneered. "Why'd I do that?" he asked. "Yer horse is twicet as big as mine."

David laughed out loud. "Not the horses, Jake. Us. A race would warm us up. Dry our clothes a little, too."

"YA GOTTA FOLLOW ME EVERPLACE I GO?"

Jake looked David over. "That'd be as dumb as racin' the horses," he said. "Ain't you noticed I'm big, and you're little?"

"I don't mind. See that tree over there? I'll race you to it and back to the horses."

After grumbling a little, Jake agreed.

The boys dropped the horses' reins over a bush and stood side by side. "Ready—set—go!" David yelled taking off as fast as he could. Let him win, a voice said. David shook his head and poured on the speed. He'd beat that big dolt if he had to sprout wings. Let Jake win! David looked over his shoulder to see who spoke. He saw only Jake, falling farther behind. After a moment's glee, he heard the voice again. Let Jake win. Then he realized God had spoken to his heart and slowed enough to let the bigger boy win.

Jake swaggered to his horse, hopped on and leered at David. "Gonna try that again, runt?"

David wanted more than anything to tell Jake he'd let

GOD HAD SPOKEN TO HIS HEART

him win, but God wouldn't like that. Besides, Jake wouldn't believe him.

"Aintcha got some sort of excuse for not runnin' fast, Davy?"

David smiled. "I don't need an excuse, Jake. You outran me, that's all." He hopped on his horse, and the two caught up with the wagon train which had moved ahead.

David rode to his family who were walking together, Pa driving the oxen on one wagon, Annie taking her turn driving the other, and Mama and Katie walking beside the wagons. David dismounted and drove Pa's oxen for a few hours, so Pa could walk with Mama.

"Who's the boy who sleeps beside you?" eighteen-year-old Annie asked. "How come he runs off when he gets up?"

David grinned. "I think he sleeps beside me because he's scared to be alone at night. He leaves when he wakes up because he hates me."

"WHO'S THE BOY WHO SLEEPS BESIDE YOU?"

WAGONS WEST

As if hearing his name mentioned, Jake appeared, jumped off his pony and walked beside Annie. He grinned at her. "Is Davy telling you how I beat him at his own game?"

"What's up?" Annie called to David ahead with the other wagon.

"He beat me in a foot race," Davy called back. Then he laughed out loud. "At least I got warmed up. How about you, Jake?"

Jake pulled back his shoulders. "Only a baby would have been cold anyways."

Annie hugged her arms against her chest as she walked along. "I've been cold all day."

Jake ripped off his filthy shirt and handed it to her. "Here, wear mine. I been sweatin' all day."

Annie shuddered and put on the dirty garment.

Jake slid off his pony. "I'll drive your oxen. You ride Princess. She'll get you warm."

"Thanks," Annie said mounting the pony. "I love riding."

"I'VE BEEN COLD ALL DAY"

WAGONS WEST

Three men coming to meet them on the trail turned and moved with the train. "Better turn back fore you get any futher," one of them said.

"Yeah," the second one chimed in. "We been most all the way to Oregon and hardly anyone can make it. People and animals dyin' like grass."

Penberry, the train captain, ordered the train on.

Soon they came to another stream—and an Indian toll bridge. They wanted 50 cents for wagons and 25 cents for people. All paid, glad to get across.

That night Jake showed up at the Moreland campsite looking somewhat cleaner—and with his hair combed. He handed Annie a piece of hard candy.

"Thank you," she said. "I'll just whack this with a knife handle, and break it so we can all share it."

"I brought it for you," Jake said.

"Thanks, but I couldn't eat such a special treat in front of my little sister and brother." She got the knife, whacked the candy until it broke into several pieces and

HE HANDED ANNIE A PIECE OF HARD CANDY

shared it with Katie, Ma, Pa, David, and Jake. The tiny slivers of candy gave everyone a taste of tangy peppermint.

The Sabbath came, but the wagons didn't stop. "How can we keep the Sabbath when we're making the oxen work so hard, and we're not going to church?" Katie asked as they walked through grassy prairie.

Pa turned from the oxen he walked beside. "The wagon train won't stop just for us, baby. God understands, but why don't we sing hymns?" The family sang together for an hour as they walked.

"Let's talk to God for awhile now," Mama suggested. "We can do it while we walk without closing our eyes." They took turns thanking Him for the sunshiny day, for loving them enough to give His only Son to die for them so they could live forever, for the Sabbath, for keeping them safe and strong, and everything they could remember.

"Let's recite scripture verses," David suggested,

"GOD UNDERSTANDS"

leading his oxen around a large bush.

When they finished, Annie began her turn driving David climbed onto Thunder's back and rode off to look around.

"I ain't never seen such a bunch of babies in my life,' Jake spat out as he rode up behind David.

"I AIN'T NEVER SEEN SUCH A BUNCH OF BABIES IN MY LIFE"

"YOU'RE TOO OLD FOR FAIRY TALES, DAVY BABY"

CHAPTER 4

David knew Jake aimed his remark at him so decided to ignore it.

"What were ya doin'? Talking to yourselves?"

"We were talking and singing to God."

"I din't see no god."

"He lives in Heaven, Jake. His Holy Spirit lives in our hearts. He hears us talk, even when we don't move our lips."

"You're too old for fairy tales, baby Davy."

"God's not a fairy tale, Jake. He's right here in my heart. He even talks to me sometimes."

Jake came alongside David, reached out and slapped Thunder hard on the rear, then sat and laughed when the big black horse took off.

David felt his face growing red with anger. *When Jake comes slinking around tonight, I'll just yell for everyone to come see the baby who's afraid to sleep alone.*

But he didn't. He wouldn't do that to anyone. Anyway, he'd discovered he liked having Jake near while he slept.

It rained all night. The next morning, the men yoked the oxen, harnessed the mules, and hooked them to the wagons. But the animals couldn't pull the wagons out of the mire. The men whipped them until the oxen bawled pitifully and the mules fell down, but they couldn't pull the wagons out.

David watched until they started whipping the animals, then sick to his stomach, he went back to his wagon and crawled up under the bonnet, which dripped water on him.

Finally, they gave up, turned the animals into the grass again and waited for the rain to stop.

The sun came out about mid-afternoon but Penberry decided to let the ground dry overnight.

The next day the oxen tried to evade the yokes. Blood ran from their necks where the rough wooden

THE MEN WHIPPED THEM

yokes had worn the hide away.

After an hour of traveling, they passed a grave. David slid off Thunder, found several handfuls of tall purple flowers and put them on the grave.

"Ha! I s'pose yer cryin' for the poor man who got kilt by Indians. Go ahead and cry, baby Davy. You'll prob'ly be next."

"Hello, Jake," David said. He walked away without looking at Jake.

Late that afternoon, David returned from a ride around the train to find Jake helping Annie pick flowers for another grave. A big mouthful of words formed in his throat, but he didn't say them. *A soft answer turneth away wrath.* "Thanks, God," David whispered. "Maybe if I stay nice, someday Jake will get nice, too."

Every day grew colder instead of warmer. David put on more and more clothes until he wore nearly everything he owned.

One day, they began hearing about people dying

"YOU'LL PROBABLY BE NEXT"

from cholera, a disease that caused people to have diarrhea and to vomit. Everyone quieted, as they worried about the dreadful sickness.

One day they reached Blue River, a landmark on The Trail. The travelers forded the river, forty feet across and about three feet deep. They took the wagons across one at a time, men wading with the oxen while others pushed the wagons.

As they met people going the other way, they learned of more cholera deaths. And graves became common along the trail. Some had been dug into—either by Indians or animals. Dead animals, mostly oxen, became common alongside The Trail.

Jake still slept beside David but usually neither spoke. One night he flopped his blanket down, wrapped up in it and turned to face David. "Know what, baby Davy? I hate to have to tell you this, but there ain't no God."

If David kept still, he'd be denying His God. He sat

THEY BEGAN HEARING ABOUT CHOLERA

up. "I'm sorry you don't know Him, Jake, but He's there. Want me to tell you about Him?"

Jake snorted. "Why waste yer time?"

"Because He loves you, Jake, and he feels awful when you don't love Him."

Jake remained quiet for so long, David almost fell asleep.

Suddenly, Jake jerked upright. "Shut up, baby Davy! I don't want to hear any more about that stuff. Got it?"

David turned over and pulled his blanket over his head.

The days never seemed to warm, and all the travelers had for fires was green willow which blew black smoke into their faces, warming the front of their bodies while their backs froze.

When the Sabbath came, the Morelands had their own little church again, singing, praying, reciting Bible verses. They liked it so well, they did it every week

"BECAUSE HE LOVES YOU"

while they traveled.

They crossed the Big Sandy River, then a few hours later, the Little Sandy. The green prairie grass looked lush against the blue sky, and the trees along the river seemed refreshing. But the trail began getting dusty.

They saw new graves and dead animals every day.

The train reached the Little Blue River and traveled along it for many days. The weather warmed and the rain came again turning the dusty trail into mud. They'd been making fifteen miles a day. Now, they tried for eight.

More graves lined The Trail; someone said man had died from measles. Finally, they left the Blue River, carrying wood and water. The guidebook said they wouldn't find any until the next day.

As the weather warmed, the land became flatter and more barren. David didn't see a tree or shrub all afternoon. He did see thirteen antelope.

He saw Jake, too. "Hey, baby Davy," Jake called.

THE GREEN PRAIRIE GRASS LOOKED LUSH

"We're goin' after them antelope. If you wanta come, I'll take care of you."

"No thanks," David called back. "I'll stay here and help Pa with the oxen." David didn't care to hunt or watch hunting. He loved animals and had enjoyed watching the graceful, light-colored antelope.

Five men and several boys took off on horses, following the antelope's tracks.

After stopping for the night at a dry camp, the men returned with five antelope lashed to their horses behind the saddles. Each family got a fourth of one. They appreciated the meat because all the perishable food they'd brought was gone and they subsisted on beans, dried peas, bacon and side meat, and biscuits.

When Jake threw his blanket down beside David's that night, he started telling about shooting the antelope.

"Be quiet," David said. "I'm tired and don't want to hear it."

"BE QUIET"

"Oooh, Davy baby don't like blood. Hoo, hoo. Sure you ain't a girl?" After that Jake never let David forget that he wasn't a real man.

One day, they entered Platte River Valley, so level they could see miles around. Following the river they climbed higher and higher.

On June 6, they reached Fort Kearney, set up by the government to guard The Trail from Indians. "We've traveled 319 miles," Pa said as they ate supper. "That's a purty good start—too far to turn back now." David thought Pa sounded satisfied.

Indians swarmed all over and around The Fort, selling buffalo robes, deerskin moccasins, and other things to the white people. Many people seemed eager to buy.

The fort was constructed of slabs of dirt cut into blocks and stacked up. They called it adobe. Seventy soldiers lived at Fort Kearney.

After everyone bought supplies, the wagon train

ON JUNE 6, THEY REACHED FORT KEARNEY

continued, following the Platte. Sometimes they had wood, sometimes they didn't. Sometimes they didn't have water or grass for the animals.

The oxen's tongues hung out of their mouths, and their eyes grew glassy with their unending task. They limped on sore feet, unused to working hard all day every day. "Can't we do something for them, Pa?" David asked.

Pa shook his head. "Sorry, Son. I don't like to see them this way either, but we gotta keep going."

One day, they had to cross the Platte which was wide and shallow with spots of quicksand. "Make sure you water all your livestock before crossing," Penberry told each driver. "If you don't, they may stop to get a drink, and the quicksand'll get 'em."

They took six wagons across at once, hooked together, with men pushing behind each wagon, and many oxen pulling together to make sure the wagons

"CAN'T WE DO SOMETHING FOR THEM, PA?"

or animals didn't get mired in the quicksand.

That night they camped near the spot where they forded the river. The animals had all the grass and water they needed and the people had wood.

After they ate, David, Annie, and Katie ran down to the river to wade. David rolled his overalls above his knees, and the girls held their skirts out of the shallow, muddy water.

As they enjoyed the cool water, Jake came tearing toward them. "Hey, baby Davy, I see yer scared to go out past your big toe." He didn't have shoes and didn't roll up his overalls, but ran past them into the water.

"Better be careful," David called.

Jake stopped, turned around and made an ugly face at David. "Yeah? What's goin' to get me? An alligator? C'mere, Annie and take my hand. I'll help you wade clean across this thing." Then a strange look crossed Jake's face, and he tried to jerk his feet from the

"I SEE YER SCARED TO GO OUT PAST YOUR BIG TOE"

sand. He struggled harder until he became frantic.
"Help!" he screamed. "I'm sinkin'!"

"HELP... I'M SINKIN!"

"HANG ON TIGHT AND PULL BACK!"

CHAPTER 5

"Jake's caught in the quicksand!" David yelled. "Quick! Take my hand, then each other's and hang on!"

Annie and Katie grabbed each other's hand, then David's. He led them toward Jake, testing the bottom with each step. It seemed solid until he came within a few steps of the terrified boy.

When he felt the bottom give, he turned half-around. "Hang on tight and pull back!" he said still moving toward Jake. "Give me your hand quick," he said quietly. Grabbing Jake's hand, he pulled backward and the girls pulled for all they were worth. David's feet tried to slip into the mire but he kept moving backward, pulling his big burden, with the girls' help.

A moment later Jake moved on his own, objecting strongly to David's pressure. He batted at David's arm. "Let loose a' me, you idiot. Whaddaya think ya are?"

When they reached the shore, Jake took off toward the corralled wagons without another word. "Well, so much for saving Jake's life," Annie said. "He's strange."

"He likes you," David said. "Know that?"

Annie laughed. "Don't be ridiculous, Dave. I'm a grown woman."

Jake came after dark that night, as usual, but unlike usual, he talked. He threw down his blanket and rolled up in it. Then he turned over, and turned over again. Finally, he jerked to a sitting position. "If you could just learn to quit butting into other people's doings, you'd sure be better off. And so would I. I'm sick of you, baby Davy."

David asked his Heavenly Father to send His Holy Spirit to help Jake be happier. Then he made a little snore as if asleep.

The next day, they passed through deep sand, nearly to the oxen's knees, along the Platte. Deep and hot. David got down from Thunder and walked with Mama

"DON'T BE RIDICULOUS, DAVE"

and the girls. The people's feet, bigger in proportion to their weight than the animals', sank in only a little over their shoes.

But Katie still objected. "I can't walk in this stuff, Papa. It hurts my feet. Can I get into the wagon and ride?"

"You can and will walk in it," Papa thundered back at her. "Look how high it comes on the oxen's legs. And they have to pull the wagon."

By evening, everyone, people and animals, struggled along, barely able to walk. David rejoiced when the wagon master called a halt for the night, two miles past Ash Hollow.

Wild roses bloomed everywhere. The delightful smell almost hid the smell of dead animals. David and Katie wandered around after supper and found a log cabin. The door opened easily so they went inside. Hundreds of sealed envelopes littered the rough wood floor.

"YOU CAN AND WILL WALK IN IT"

"Let's open some," Katie said.

"You don't bother other people's mail," David said. "The people who left them probably hoped someone would deliver them."

The next morning, Jake called David away from his breakfast. When David followed, he discovered Jake had an armload of freshly picked pink roses. They smelled almost good enough to eat.

Jake shoved the flowers at David. "Here. Take these to Annie."

"Why?"

"'Cause I said so. Git going, baby Davy."

"I'm not your servant, Jake. If you want someone to have them, take them yourself." He forced the flowers back into Jake's surprised arms.

Jake backed off and looked at David with surprise. Throwing the flowers onto the ground, he stomped them to shreds, then marched off.

The wagon train stayed in deep sand and dust which

JAKE BACKED OFF

got into everyone's eyes, making them sore and running. Pus ran from the animals eyes down their face. They didn't go far each day.

They camped on the banks of the Platte River each night and bugs came out by the thousands. Some bit some didn't. One kind of large black bugs called dor bugs, came out of holes in the ground at night. They didn't bite but marched across people's faces all night long. Jake woke David several times each night beating bugs from his face and body and stomping the ground trying to get the bugs. As soon as he lay back down, the bugs began marching again. David tried to sleep through it all.

The roads gradually grew firmer. Beautiful flowers bloomed, but many more graves appeared.

They met "turnarounds" almost every day. Turnarounds were what they called the men coming back on The Trail. They always seemed to have bad news. David hated to see them coming.

MANY MORE GRAVES APPEARED

One day, they met a scruffy-looking group. "There
bad Indians ahead," the black-whiskered one sai
"Tried to put some arrows through us, but we was to
fast for 'em."

David watched all day but saw nothing. Suddenl
the next evening, Indians swarmed over the enti
train. The train members readied their guns. Th
Indians made motions telling the white people the
wanted their guns. When the whites refused, th
Indians grabbed their bows from their backs.

Penberry raised his rifle and shot into the air. Sever;
other men did the same.

At the sound, the Indians turned their ponies, gav
loud yells and rode off into the darkening dusk.

David still shook when he rolled into his blanke
Jake didn't say a word. After that, the men took turn
guarding the train at night.

On June 13, they reached Chimney Rock. Some c
the people rode horses the three miles to it while other

"THERE'S BAD INDIANS AHEAD"

rested with the animals. The gigantic rock looked like a rounded mountain with a tall chimney on top. David checked Pa's guide book. "This thing's 250 feet high," he said. "The top 75 feet is called the chimney." The soft rock, like limestone, had hundreds of names carved into it. The young people climbed up about 200 feet and added their names. David had a hard time finding a place for his.

As he climbed down, he noticed a freshly carved heart with Jake and Annie inside.

That night David told Jake that Annie was way too old for him. "She's eighteen, Jake. Katie's more your age. She's thirteen."

"Aw, shuddup. Whadda you know?" Jake answered, flipping his back to David.

A few days later, they reached the bluffs: high, steep cliffs on each side of the road. Some of the bluffs reached 500 feet high. Scott's Bluff seemed to be the highest, also the only one the guidebook named. Often,

THEY REACHED THE BLUFFS

the train traveled late to find water for the animals.

"I'm sick of hard bread," Katie said one night. "We haven't had anything else to eat for a long time."

Mama put her arm around Katie and pulled her close. "We'll all be glad to have something else, honey. As soon as we find wood, we'll cook some beans and bacon." She pushed Katie's light hair back from her round face.

"We're all tired of hard bread, Katie," Papa said. "But the animals are thankful to eat anything they can. We should be too."

After a few more days of hard travel they arrived at Fort Laramie, the second army fort set up to protect The Trail, 650 miles from Independence. As at Fort Kearney, Indians and whites ran back and forth everywhere. Some walked, some rode horses or ponies. Everyone seemed to be selling or buying. The wagon train stopped only long enough to restock their supplies then moved on.

"WE'RE ALL TIRED OF HARD BREAD, KATIE"

Soon, they came to ruts in The Trail that were so deep they reached the oxen's bellies.

The weather grew stiflingly hot, even when they could see the Black Hills with snow-covered peaks. After crossing several small rivers and streams, they followed the Platte again.

They had wood to cook with, but the bugs got into everything, even the pots of food as they cooked. Mama dipped out the bugs before she poured the beans into dishes. Then David had to pick the new bugs out before he could eat.

He thought he'd never be able to eat after all that, but he felt so hungry, the food tasted good.

One evening, word passed around the camp that a man had fallen sick. People thought he might have cholera. Fear hung in the air so strongly, David could almost see it. David wondered if he'd be next—and if he'd die.

DAVID WONDERED IF HE'D BE NEXT

"YEAH...MAMA'S LITTLE HELPER"

CHAPTER 6

The next day, the man wasn't able to travel, so the train didn't move.

"Hey, baby Davy," Jake called coming into the Moreland camp. "Wanta go find some rabbits and sage hens?"

"Sorry," David said, cringing at the thought of killing a helpless animal. "I have to gather sage brush for Mama's fire."

"Yeah. Mama's little helper." Jake plodded off, his gun pointed at the ground.

A while later, Pa came into camp looking disturbed. "An ox just died," he said tersely. "I had no idea he was in that bad shape. God created valiant animals when He made oxen. They work until they drop." He hesitated a moment. "Another's bad, too. Why don't you find some grass for him, Dave."

David found a little grass but far from enough.

The men returned from the hunt with many rabbits and sage hens, two for each wagon.

The next morning, the sick man seemed better, and the animals desperately needed food, so the wagon train moved on. They left the Platte for good and camped near Willow Springs. The sick man still lived, but the ox died.

The Sweetwater Mountain tops glistened with ice and snow while the weather turned from hot to scorching.

David rolled his pants to his knees and his shirt sleeves to his elbows, hoping for a cool breeze.

They passed Alkali Lake which conisted of several large ponds with water resembling lye. The animals tried desperately to get to the lakes which went on for several miles, but the men restrained them from the poisonous water.

Finally, they reached Independence Rock, standing alone in the Sweetwater Valley—separated from other

THE WEATHER TURNED FROM HOT TO SCORCHING

mountains. The immense granite rock lay 500 feet long, 200 feet wide and 250 feet high, one of nature's most magnificent structures. Thousands of names appeared on the rock, painted on with tar. David, Katie, and Annie, walked away with their knife unused and their names unwritten. The knife couldn't cut granite.

Before they left Independence Rock, the sick man died. They buried him right in The Trail. After a small ceremony and prayer, they moved on. Wagon after wagon ran over the fresh grave.

"Why do we run over the poor man?" Katie cried.

Papa gathered his youngest child into his arms. "Because animals and Indians dig up graves," he said. "The animals eat the people, and the Indians steal the clothes. We tried to hide the grave by running over it."

Two men managed to shoot a lone buffalo, and the train stayed in camp an extra day while the women dried the meat so it wouldn't spoil.

"ANIMALS AND INDIANS DIG UP GRAVES"

Almost as soon as the train started again, they came to the Sweetwater River, a beautiful clear, cold stream, sixty feet across and three feet deep. When told they had to ford it, David, Katie, and Annie made a game of it. Many other young people, and some not so young, joined in the fun. They waded, swam, splashed water on each other, yelled and laughed until they forgot for a little while where they were and the hardships they endured. David, a strong swimmer, swam the width of the river several times.

"Hey!" Katie yelled. "Here comes Jake on his pony. Let's pull him off."

Jake fought hard but they finally jerked him into the cold water. "Help!" he yelled. "You idiots! Get me out of here. I can't swim!"

David laughed and held out a hand which Jake grabbed. "Put your feet down," David said. "The water's only waist deep."

Jake put his feet down but refused to enjoy the water.

THEY MADE A GAME OF IT

"Get my horse!" he demanded. But the pony stood on the far bank waiting. Jake angrily waded across.

Even after the heat grew intense, the memory of the cold water kept David cool most of the day.

That evening a young man appeared in the Moreland camp. "Is Annie here?" he asked.

Annie came from the other side of the wagon. "I'm here," she said.

"Hello Annie," he said. "Remember me? I'm Mark Mathis, the one you tried to drown this morning when we crossed the river."

Annie laughed. "I remember. I always remember the people I drown." Soon, the two went walking around the corralled wagons.

Mark stayed for Bible reading and prayer.

"Who's the geezer who hung around here tonight?" Jake grouched when he came to sleep.

"Just a friend of Annie's," David said. He fell asleep while Jake named every reason why Mark wasn't fit to

MARK STAYED FOR BIBLE READING AND PRAYER

be called a human being.

One evening, two more oxen died. The next morning, two more couldn't get up. "We'll have to leave them," Pa said. "Let's hope the good Lord gives them strength after we're gone. But now, we don't have enough oxen left to pull the two wagons. We'll have to cut one in two and make a cart."

The train waited while David, Jake, Mark, and several other men helped Papa cut off the front wheels and most of the wagon bed.

Mama and Annie sorted through their things, tossing everything they possibly could beside The Trail among previous wagons' discards. Furniture, clothes, empty food barrels, chains, and other things.

"Mark," Annie said at one point, "you're supposed to be lifting that wagon, not sitting on it."

A little later Mark wandered over to Annie. "You're supposed to be tossing things onto the trail, not collecting more stuff," he kidded.

"YOU'RE SUPPOSED TO BE LIFTING THAT WAGON"

"I am throwing things out," she replied laughing. "Now, you go back over there and get busy."

Every time Mark and Annie laughed together, Jake looked madder. Finally, he dropped the corner of the wagon he'd been holding and stomped away.

"There's still room for Annie and me to sleep in the cart," Katie said. "So it's all right."

"If you have to leave the rest of it you can sleep on the ground with me," David offered. The girls told him no thanks.

David took the ox whip from Mama and drove the oxen until nooning.

A few days later, they saw the Green River Mountains in the distance, their peaks reaching heaven. They began climbing into the Rocky Mountains with steep, dusty roads and deep sand. Another ox gave out. Reluctantly, Pa left it beside The Trail.

Other wagons in the train had the same trouble. More and more animals died. The stench became so

"YOU CAN SLEEP ON THE GROUND WITH ME!"

terrible the people could hardly eat.

"Go upstream and find some good clean water," Ma instructed David one evening as it grew dark. She handed him a jug.

Walking upstream he kept finding dead oxen lying in the water. After walking a long way he decided the water would be all right and dipped the jug full.

When Mama called the family to supper of beans and biscuits, he kept thinking of all the stinking oxen around, even in the stream.

The next morning Mama asked for more water so he went upstream to the place he'd gotten it last night. As he dipped, he glanced upstream. A decaying horse lay half in the water. Dumping the water back, he returned without water.

One day, they reached the peak of one of the Rocky Mountains. They found gravel, grass and sagebrush. Not a tree was to be seen except stunted scrubs, their tops covered with snow.

HE KEPT FINDING DEAD OXEN IN THE WATER

David and his sisters scraped off the crust and ate the snow by handfuls.

Dust blew hard all the time, leaving everyone with runny noses and sore throats and eyes. Mama handed them large handkerchiefs. "Here, put these around your heads covering your eyes and nose. You can see through, and it'll protect you some."

The oxen limped painfully along, heads drooping, tongues hanging from their mouths, moaning. Besides being terribly overworked, the animals never had enough grass anymore.

One day, the captain stopped the train in the early afternoon. "This here's known as Southpass. We're in Oregon Territory now, folks. Sublette Cutoff takes off here, savin' two days travelin', but it's even worse than The Trail which is pretty bad here. We go that way, we're sure to lose more oxen. I say we stay on The Trail as our animals are in bad shape already. How about the rest of you?"

THE CAPTAIN STOPPED THE TRAIN

"WE'D BETTER REST THE ANIMALS A DAY..."

CHAPTER 7

Most agreed with the captain. Jake tried to get his father to take the cutoff, but he refused.

After traveling a few days, the captain called another meeting. "We'd better rest the animals a day here because we have 45 miles with no water or grass. It's gonna be tough, so we'll travel all day and night."

After resting the extra day, they started at four o'clock the next morning and traveled hard, stopping briefly for dinner at noon. They stopped for an hour at dusk and at midnight for an hour's rest. At two o'clock in the morning, they came to a steep and dangerous hill. The animal handlers walked beside their animals guiding them slowly and carefully down. The walkers stayed behind the wagons.

The worn-out group stopped at five o'clock in the morning to rest and eat breakfast. When they went on they left two more oxen. The stumbling, moaning, gaunt animals remaining brought tears to David's eyes.

The train reached Green River at mid-afternoon. When the oxen smelled the water, they became so excited the men couldn't stop them from dragging the wagons into the river. They dipped their entire heads into the water in their desperation for a drink.

The people were also glad to have the long trek finished, to rest, and let the animals drink and eat the plentiful grass. Annie, Mark, Katie, and David walked back to the river. Trees grew on the banks, flowers bloomed nearby, and ripe strawberries hid in the shiny-leaved plants. They picked enough for a bowl for each of them and also bowlfuls for their parents.

"I see they got the babies pickin' berries," Jake's familiar voice growled behind them.

David whirled around to face Jake. A sharp retort formed in his mind, but the words didn't come out. "Yes, taste them," he said, holding out a small handful.

Jake swatted the bottom of David's hand, sending

A SHARP RETORT FORMED IN HIS MIND

berries flying. David's right hand clenched. He wante
to pound Jake. But he bent over to find more of the tin
red berries.

David thought Jake would leave, but the larger bo
hung around saying nothing.

As they picked berries, David noticed some peopl
playing and yelling up the river. They moved close
still picking. Jake stayed behind David.

"Hey!" David said. "Those are Indians." Protect us
Father. Make them friendly. Help us be kind to them
too. As they watched, one Indian boy pushed som
kind of a hoop until it rolled fast. The others bega
throwing stones through the center.

"Those people are good!" Annie whispered.

The Indians gave a shout, and about twenty ran at th
white people.

"Run, David!" Katie screamed.

But David knew they could never outrun the fleet
footed people storming toward them. He grabbed hi

THE INDIANS GAVE A SHOUT

sisters' hands and stood straight.

The Indians stopped ten feet from the whites and signalled for them to come and throw stones through the hoops with them.

David noticed Jake about a hundred feet back, ready to retreat farther.

Some of the Indian young people dressed in ragged and faded overalls and shirts, some dressed in soft buckskin. All wore moccasins.

After waiting a few minutes, a tall Indian boy stepped forward and made motions of throwing rocks. Then, he motioned for David to come with them.

David decided to go. Thank You, Father. "Come on," he told the others, "let's go."

Soon, the hoop roller ran in front of them and gave the hoop a hard push. The Indians stooped and grabbed handfuls of rocks. David, Mark, Katie, and Annie did the same. Katie's and Annie's rocks made it about halfway to the hoop. Several Indian stones shot through

DAVID DECIDED TO GO

as it continued rolling. David pulled back his right arm and threw as straight as possible. The rock passed through the moving circle.

A yell of approval came from the Indians.

"Aw, it ain't that good," a miserable voice said into David's ear. Jake picked up several rocks and pelted them toward the hoop. Two fell short and one veered off to the right.

The Indians won every game.

"It'd take a fool to waste time on such a dumb game," Jake grumbled before running back down the river.

David, Mark, and the girls waved to the Indians as they left. David hadn't had such a good time since they had left Independence. Beating Jake so thoroughly hadn't hurt his feelings either.

When Jake arrived to sleep beside David that night, he acted extra surly. "Why'd you hafta go an' take the only level spot?" he growled.

"WHY'D YOU HAFTA GO AN' TAKE THE ONLY LEVEL SPOT?"

David moved his blanket over five feet. Neither boy said anymore for awhile. "Who's that dumb feller at the river with you tonight?" Jake finally asked.

David smiled to himself. He'd been wondering what Jake thought about Mark. "That was Mark Mathis," he whispered. "He's Annie's friend."

"Ain't neither. She ain't that dumb—to take up with someone like that."

"Jake," David whispered, "she's too old for you. Why are you so unhappy?"

Jake jerked upright. "Who said I was?"

"Jesus loves you, Jake. And He feels sad when you're sad. Want to talk to Him with me? If you tell Him why you're so sad, He'll make you happy."

"I'd like to know how He'd do that. Think he'd bring Ma back? Or make Pa remember I'm around?"

"I don't know how He'll do it, Jake, but He will. Let's tell Him."

"Forget it, baby Davy. Only babies believe fairy tales."

"WHO SAID I WAS?"

"Good night, Jake." Jake didn't reply.

David, Jake and other scouts fanned out in all directions from The Trail, searching for the precious stuff that would keep the animals alive. When they found grass, the train stopped until the animals ate it all or filled up.

The train continued on over hilly and dangerous roads. More oxen died, or couldn't get up. Some dropped dead while pulling.

On the Fourth of July, a day usually set apart for celebration, fierce winds came up. They tore the tents to pieces and forced the men to tie the wagons together with ropes. While waiting for the winds to die down many people lightened their loads even more. They broke up trunks and used them for firewood. They left tinware, baskets, axes, and shovels. Deserted wagons, carts, dressers, and other furniture lined The Trail, along with carcasses of animals and many graves.

FIERCE WINDS CAME UP

One day, after climbing dangerous and wearing hills, the train stopped at noon on Bear River to let the women wash clothes, and the oxen gather strength.

Lots of flowers and strawberries grew along the river. David soon discovered they'd made camp beside an Indian gathering with thirty wigwams. Make them friendly, Father. The Indians came around, watching everything they did, making everyone nervous, but they didn't bother anyone.

The next day, they passed through trees, making the first shade they'd had on the trip. They began ascending Bear Mountain and following Bear River.

During nooning that day, two hundred Indians surrounded the wagons.

TWO HUNDRED INDIANS SURROUNDED THE WAGONS

THEY COULDN'T UNDERSTAND HIM

CHAPTER 8

Braves, squaws, children, dogs, and ponies approached the wagons and surrounded them. Some spoke a little English, so word soon traveled through the wagons that the Indians were begging.

Most families found something to give the Indians who went away with their new treasures. David longed to tell the Indians about the great Father God who loved them so much, but they couldn't understand him.

A few days later, they reached Soda Springs which were really nine or ten springs where clear water sparkled, boiled, and bubbled. Some of the springs shot steam into the air making small geysers. The pilgrims soon learned that adding a little acid and sugar made good drinks. The spring water also made biscuits rise high and fluffy. The women washed clothes in the hot water, the first time they'd used hot water since they had left Independence.

The train passed Myers Cutoff where the people heading for California left the Oregon Trail.

David took Thunder down the California trail a bit to see what it was like.

"Goin' to Californy?" Jake's gravelly voice asked.

David felt too good to let Jake upset him. "No, just seeing how it feels to head for California. I'm glad I'm going to Oregon."

"I sure ain't. If you was goin' to Californy, I'd be rid of you right now."

David desperately wanted to ask Jake who'd watch over him while he slept, but he didn't.

The next few days, the train moved through a lava field with fine dust three inches deep. Lava—volcano flow that had turned to rock—lay everywhere, making The Trail almost impassable. In some places, the rock was 15 feet high. With the dust, it made the road resemble a huge ash heap. Grass had grown over the rock in some places. The grass and holes in the rock

"IF YOU WAS GOIN' TO CALIFORNY, I'D BE RID OF YOU"

made good retreats for small animals.

The dust on The Trail blew so badly David couldn't see the wagon in front of his. Sometimes, he couldn't even see his own oxen.

One evening, Annie and Katie found June berries beside a gurgling creek. "They're growing on low bushes," they explained to David. "Come help us pick some so Mama can make a pie."

Mama made three pies. "You go find two families that need pies," she told the three young Morelands. "God says to share our blessings."

The three went around the circle talking to many of the travelers.

"We found the ones who need pies," they told Mama when they returned. "The Mackies have five children and not much food anymore."

"Fine," Mama said. "You can take a pie to them. What about the other one?"

David hung his head, but the girls weren't embar-

"FINE...YOU CAN TAKE A PIE TO THEM"

rassed. "Jake and his father have hardly anything," Katie said. "They need help more than anyone."

So the two girls and David took the first pie to the Mackies, and the second to Jake and his father. Jake was alone and looked longingly at the crusty dessert. "Why'd we want that thing?" he asked in a coarse voice.

"Because we like you," Annie said, handing it to him. "And we made it just for you."

He quickly put on a new face and shoved his hair back. Then he accepted the pie with thanks. "If you made it, I'll take it," he said. "I thought for a minute baby Davy made it, and that wouldn't be good."

Finally, one day they arrived at Fort Hall on the Snake River, the last big fort on The Trail. The guidebook said this was thirteen hundred miles from Independence. Fort Hall was built from adobe, like Kearney and Laramie. The land around the fort was wet and marshy. David couldn't wait to move on.

"WE MADE IT JUST FOR YOU"

Abandoned wagons, parts of wagons, household goods, dead animals, and live Indians—lots of Indians—crowded around the big, ugly place.

The tired company didn't find soldiers there anymore, but they found food at a reasonable price. Many of the people bought flour, beans, side meat, and other staples.

Two days later, David heard a strange sound in the early afternoon. As they traveled, it grew louder until it roared loudly; a sound he'd never heard.

When David took over driving the oxen, Papa got out his guide book. A few minutes later, the worried look on his face turned into a wide smile. "We're hearing the American Falls," he said. "Says here it can be heard for seven miles."

As they traveled, the sound grew so loud, they had to shout to hear each other.

Jake appeared on the scene. David had never seen anyone so white, or eyes so big and wide. "Whaddaya

DAVID HAD NEVER SEEN ANYONE SO WHITE

think it could be?" he asked. "And where is it? I been lookin' all afternoon."

David laughed. "Don't worry, Jake. It's a big waterfall ahead. "We'll probably camp near it tonight. Think you'll be able to sleep?"

The strain lines in Jake's face eased away, and he heaved a long, deep sigh. Then the hard look returned. "I knew what it was, baby Davy. Thought I'd better make sure you did." He kicked his horse hard in the sides and raised a dust, leaving the family behind.

All through the afternoon, the hot, deep sand came over and into their shoes making walking painful. Finally they reached the falls, where cascades of water fell 40 feet over large irregular rocks. David had never seen nor heard anything so vast. "Thank You for making such wonderful things, God," he said loudly, knowing no one but God could hear in the roar of the falling tons of water.

The sound slowly grew softer as they moved past

CASCADES OF WATER FELL 40 FEET OVER LARGE ROCKS

through deepening sand. Soon, The Trail disappeared into the immense rocks to the right. On the left, steep banks ended fifteen feet below, beside the river. For the first time, there was no place to go. No place at all.

THERE WAS NO PLACE TO GO...NO PLACE AT ALL.

"WE'RE GOING TO LET THE WAGONS DOWN WITH ROPES"

CHAPTER 9

The wagon train stopped and the men all gathered around the captain.

"Will we have to go back to Independence?" Katie asked.

Mama shook her head. "Lots of wagon trains have passed this way before. The men will know what to do."

David had picked up the guidebook. "I know what we're going to do," he said proudly. "We're going to let the wagons down the bank with ropes."

"No, we ain't," a gruff voice spoke from behind. David spun around to find Jake once again looking frightened. "You go puttin' those wagons over the edge and you'll wreck every one of them."

David looked ahead again where The Trail ended at the steep rocks. "Well, it's go over the banks or go back the way we came."

Pa came hurrying back. "We're lowering the wagons over the bank," he said. "It'll most likely take the rest of the afternoon and maybe into the night. Right now we're gathering all the ropes we can find."

"Can I help, Pa?"

"Yeah. Go to each wagon and collect all the rope you can." Pa gave David a grateful glance. "Thanks, Son." He hurried away with the rope he'd found in their wagon.

"Want to help?" David asked Jake.

"I don't do baby stuff." He turned to Annie who sat on a box she'd pulled from the wagon. "Wanna go take a look?"

She stood up. "No. I'll help David find more ropes."

Annie and David took turns stopping at every other wagon. When they had all the rope they could hold, they carried it to the men, then returned for more.

When the men had everything collected, they took ten yoke of oxen, stationed them about thirty feet back

"THANKS SON"

from the bank and fastened the ropes to them. Then they secured the ropes to the first wagon which had been pulled to the edge. The oxen holding the wagon, backed up slowly, putting the weight of the wagon on the yokes as the men let it down the edge, carefully and right side up. In less than half an hour, the first wagon stood on the river bank, none the worse for wear.

"We'll have to hurry up or we'll be working all night," Pa said. As they learned what they were doing, they gained speed. The last wagon wheels touched the riverbank before midnight.

The weary men took the exhausted oxen to grass and went to bed.

A few days later, they camped beside a busy, little stream where they found currants. Annie and Katie joined the other girls picking them while the women made pastry shells, and whatever they planned to cook them with.

Jake ran into the camp. "Baby Davy, there's a

THE FIRST WAGON STOOD ON THE RIVER BANK

million trout in that there crik. Grab yer pole and come on."

By the time Jake and David reached the stream, many boys and men had their hooks in the water.

"That ugly feller botherin' Annie anymore?" Jake asked as they fished.

"Yeah. He comes over most every night."

Jake threw his pole into the water and stormed off. David pulled it out.

In less than an hour, every family in the camp had enough fish for supper. David took Jake's pole and four large fish to Jake and his father.

The currant pastries and the fish tasted like manna from heaven after eating dried beans for so long.

Later that evening, Jake appeared. "I gotta talk to Annie," he told Mama.

When Annie came, Jake acted mysterious. "I gotta show you somethin'," he said. "Come with me."

Annie looked at David. "Sure. Come on, Dave."

JAKE THREW HIS POLE INTO THE WATER

"Get outta here," Jake snapped at David.

Annie stopped short. "He has to come if I do, Jake. You see, I don't know you very well."

Jake looked mad, then cheered up. "All right. Just keep yer mouth shut, baby Davy." He walked on with Annie following, then David. After a distance lay between them and the other campers Jake pulled something from his pocket and handed it to Annie.

She looked the three or four ounce light-brownish stone over. "What is it?" she asked.

Jake looked the happiest David had ever seen him. "It's gold," he said.

David moved closer. "Are you sure?" he asked. "I've never seen raw gold before."

"I'm thrilled for you," Annie said. She handed it back, but Jake shook his shaggy black head.

"I got it for you," he said. "Found it in the edge of the river. Just for you." No amount of talking convinced him to take the stone back. Finally, he ran off.

"IT'S GOLD"

What do I do now?" she asked David. "I can't keep this thing."

David laughed out loud. "I guess you have to. At least for now."

In the following days, the roads grew almost impassable. Loose rocks made the oxen stumble time after time. They staggered along in the deep dust, coughing at every step.

People fell many times, cutting themselves on the sharp rocks. Thousands of acres of sagebrush spread before the slowly moving wagon train. The hot sun burned the grass, the people, and the oxen who hung their heads as their tongues dangled from open mouths.

One day, Indians began following the train. Word spread throughout the train, terrifying everyone. Neither the oxen nor the people could move faster, so they continued slowly onward. The day wore on and the Indians stayed behind.

"Whadda ya think they're gonna do?" Jake asked.

"WHADDA YA THINK THEY'RE GONNA DO?"

David shook his head. "I don't know, but I know how to be safe." He looked up. "Thanks for loving us so much, God. You know whether those Indians following us mean us harm. Be with us all, Father, so that no one gets hurt." Almost as soon as David finished praying, the Indians turned and went back the way they'd come. "Thank You, Father," he whispered. "You're a great God, know that?"

"How'd you do that?" Jake asked. "What did you do?"

David couldn't hold back a grin. "I told you He loves us, Jake. If we give ourselves to Him and trust Him completely, He'll always take care of us."

"Sure. I know you did something, baby Davy. What was it?"

No matter how much he talked, David couldn't convince Jake that God did it, not him.

They went two and three days with no food for the oxen several times. The people had only hard bread

"HOW'D YOU DO THAT?"

which was much better than nothing.

The heat grew more intense as the days passed. Heat waves rose from the oxen's backs. More oxen died, more wagons had to be turned into carts, and more valuables had to be left beside the road.

Whenever the scouts found grass, the train stopped while the animals ate.

The sun burned with intense heat. No tree or even a bush grew in the barren wilderness to offer a bit of shade to the worn people or animals.

Sometimes, they stayed in camp through the days and traveled at night, but the scouts were more likely to miss a patch of grass at night. The exhausted animals couldn't go far anymore, so they had many short traveling days.

One day, they came to a narrow path between a high hill and a river. David rode Thunder over the dangerous part first then got off and watched, hoping he could help somehow.

DAVID RODE THUNDER OVER THE DANGEROUS PART

WAGONS WEST

The wagons crept across, one at a time, the handlers walking ahead.

Most of the wagons had safely crossed when one tumbled over the bank into the river, taking its three yoke of oxen with it.

The men rushed to the spot but couldn't unyoke the oxen from the crushed wagon. The gallant animals drowned in the swirling water.

The rest crossed safely and a quiet group made camp. Another family took in the middle-aged couple who lost their wagon, belongings, and oxen.

"Purty good, warn't it?" Jake's rough voice asked that night when he dropped his blanket beside David.

"What was good?" David asked.

"That wagon goin' over the bank."

"PURTY GOOD, WARN'T IT?"

"SOMETIMES, I DON'T LIKE YOU AT ALL!"

CHAPTER 10

"Jake, did you see those poor animals struggling to get out of their yokes?"

"Yeah," Jake said. "Warn't that somethin'!"

David felt like throwing up. "What's the matter with you, Jake?" he snapped. "Sometimes I don't like you at all." He wrapped the blanket tighter around himself, turned over and shut his eyes. Then he realized what he'd said. How could he? After all these miles of being kind to Jake no matter what, he had to go and wreck it all now. *Forgive me, Father. I don't deserve it, but please give me another chance to help Jake. Thank You, Father. I ask in Jesus' name. Amen.*

The train had good roads to Catherine Creek and a refreshing shower one afternoon. Nearly everyone on the train ran and danced in the rain. Even the oxen perked up some.

One evening, they learned that twelve people in a

nearby camp were sick. Some were seriously ill. Neither wagon train had a doctor, but they thought the people had cholera.

The wagon train plodded along day after day in the burning sun. The desolate and barren land seemed able to grow only sagebrush which the cattle couldn't eat.

Finally, they reached the Malheur River with its clean, fresh water, and grass everywhere. The train stayed two extra days to let the livestock eat and drink.

When they moved again, they reached the Snake River late in the afternoon, then left it for good.

That afternoon, the train overtook another train that had stopped for some reason. David pulled Thunder to a stop and watched a crowd of people.

"Looks like something's going on," he whispered to Annie who stood beside him and Thunder.

"I think they're having a trial," she whispered back.

As they watched, a group of men walked off about two hundred feet and talked for ten minutes. Then they

"I THINK THEY'RE HAVING A TRIAL"

returned. One of them faced the tall straight man who'd been running the meeting. "We, the jury, find the defendant guilty of stealing two horses and one cow," he said loud and clear.

"In that case I sentence you, Herbert Rice, to be hanged by the neck until dead."

Immediately, four men grabbed the defendant and shoved him onto a tall cream-colored horse. Then, they led the horse to a tree where two more men tied a rope to an overhanging branch. They leaned over and put a loop around the man's neck as he sat on the horse.

Then, before David knew what was happening, someone hit the horse's backside hard with an ox whip. The horse jumped ten feet, jerking the man from its back. The rope caught the man before he hit the ground.

David closed his eyes, turned Thunder and touched his sides with his feet. The horse took off at a fast trot. When they'd put some distance between them and the

"I SENTENCE YOU, HERBERT RICE TO BE HANGED UNTIL DEAD"

other people, David stopped Thunder, slid off, and threw up.

"Oh God," he said out loud. "Why is life so awful? People die of cholera. That's awful. Then people kill each other. What a mess your beautiful world is in, Father." He sat on the ground for awhile then got up, mounted Thunder, and caught up with the train which had moved on.

The train reached Burnt River that night. The river was named from the black and burned appearance of the hills and mountains around.

That night when Jake kept turning over in his blanket, David knew he wanted to talk. He lay still and waited.

"Whatcha think of that hanging today?" Jake finally asked.

David almost told him to shut up. He didn't want to hear Jake talk about how good it was. But he didn't answer.

"WHAT A MESS YOUR BEAUTIFUL WORLD IS IN, FATHER"

"Did ya see that feller wiggle on the end of that rope?"

Jake sounded upset about the hanging, but still David didn't answer.

"Well, how come yore God lets people kill each other?"

David couldn't keep quiet any longer. "God doesn't want people to kill each other," he said. "But people don't listen to Him. He wants people to love each other and be kind to each other."

Jake grunted out an ugly sound. "Yeah," he said. "Like you always are. Little angel, baby Davy." Neither said another word.

Something awakened David in the middle of the night and across the valley he saw a grass fire in the mountains. "Jake, wake up," he whispered. Jake didn't stir. David shook his arm. "Jake, wanna see something?"

Jake struggled to wake up and finally caught sight of

"HE WANTS PEOPLE TO LOVE EACH OTHER"

the fire. Jumping to his feet, he started yelling. "Let's get out of here!"

David jumped up, too, and grabbed Jake. "It's all right," he said. "It's way over on the mountain." Finally, he got Jake back into bed, and the boys watched the fire for awhile.

The next morning, Jake acted meaner than usual.

"Why'd you have to go and wake me up?" he snarled. "I seen lots of grass fires. They ain't nothin'."

Never again, David thought. Never again would he try to befriend the nasty boy. But before the day ended, David wanted to help Jake understand God's love.

The next day, the wagons creaked as the oxen trudged along with sore feet, sore eyes, and sore shoulders that were so thin their bones and ribs stuck out; each of their backbones looked like a big snake lying on top of them.

Vultures blackened the carcasses along the trail. Screaming their indignation about being bothered,

"LET'S GET OUT OF HERE!"

they left their meals while the train passed.

Dust covered the roads for the next days, but grass and water for people and animals were plentiful. The Blue Mountains stood tall in the distance covered with tall trees. One afternoon, it hailed just before making camp, then rained all evening. David felt so cold, he thought he'd freeze.

They began to see miles and miles of burned off vegetation. "The Indians do this to make the white man go back where he came from," Pa told David. When they reached Powder River, they met people from Oregon City coming to meet friends and relatives.

"We're almost there," David said to Mama.

She shook her head. "We still have the Blue Mountains to cross and also the Cascade Mountains. I hear they're both animal and man killers."

Leaving Powder River, going to Grande Ronde, rocks nearly obliterated The Trail. Small rocks, big rocks, smooth rocks, sharp rocks. Several oxen fell to

"WE'RE ALMOST THERE"

the ground when rocks slipped under their feet. Mules fared better, being more sure-footed.

Luxuriant grass grew in the Grande Ronde (French for Great River) Valley. Wagon trains by the dozens camped nearby that night. Indians, cattle, ponies, and horses brought the valley to life.

The Indians, Cayuse, and Nez Perce were friendly and all wanted to "swap" with the "white man." Most had ponies or cattle they wanted to trade for old clothes or most anything.

One old Indian had an old squaw he wanted to trade for a horse. David didn't see anyone trade for the squaw.

David felt a hand on his shoulder and found Jake behind him. "Come with me," Jake said softly. "I seen somethin' I want."

David followed until Jake approached a huge Indian who had several large salmon hanging on some kind of stick. Jake motioned to the largest fish. The Indian

JAKE MOTIONED TO THE LARGEST FISH

pointed to Jake's shoes. When Jake finally understood, he nodded, took off his shoes and handed them to the man. The red man took the large fish from the pole and handed it to Jake.

"What you going to do for shoes?" David asked as the boys returned to their wagon train, with Jake carrying the heavy salmon.

"Aw, them was just extra shoes I had," Jake said.

David didn't argue, though he knew better. When they reached David's family's wagons, Jake stopped, too. "Where's Annie?" he asked Katie, who ran up to see the big fish.

Annie appeared from somewhere. "What a huge fish!" she said. "Where'd you get it?"

Jake nodded over his shoulder. "Caught it in the river over there." He shoved it into her hands. "It's yours," he said. "I caught it for you." Suddenly shy, he took off without another word, lifting his bare feet carefully over rocks and briars.

"AW, THEM WAS JUST EXTRA SHOES I HAD"

Annie shoved the fish into David's arms. "Yucchh. You take it, Dave. Why would Jake catch a fish for me?"

"YUCCHH! YOU TAKE IT DAVE"

"I TRIED TO TELL HIM, BUT HE THINKS HE'S GROWN UP"

CHAPTER 11

David almost laughed when Annie wondered why Jake gave her the big salmon. "I told you he's sweet on you." he said.

"But he's just a boy, younger than you!"

"I tried to tell him, but he thinks he's grown up."

Two days later, the train started into the Blue Mountains which seemed delightful after the days of burning heat in the desert. There were real trees, big trees, to provide shade.

David barely had a chance to enjoy the trees before he realized the Blue Mountains were impassable. The hills seemed straight up—and straight down. But they had to cross them!

The oxen dug their feet into the trail, their breath choking in their throats. Wild-eyed and straining every worn out muscle in their gaunt bodies, they struggled heroically up the first steep hill.

WAGONS WEST

Great eagles swooped above them as they climbed high into the mountains.

When they reached the top, they stopped for the night with plenty of grass, water and wood. The animals and people were almost too tired to eat.

The next morning, a half-dozen men approached the Moreland wagon with a huge ox dragging a tree behind him. "We'll hook this tree behind your wagon to slow it down," they told Pa. "You take the oxen down slow and easy so they won't fall, and the wagon won't turn over, and we'll keep the wagon behind."

David walked on the other side of the oxen from Pa. They talked quietly to the nervous animals, calming them. The men hooked the tree onto the wagon, so the branches caught on the ground, holding it back. "Go, but take it easy," a man called to Pa. As they started, a loud yell caused the oxen to jump five feet.

David looked back to see Jake perched on one of the tall limbs, riding the tree down the hill. "Yahoo!" Jake

"YAHOO!"

yelled. "Git up there."

"You get off there," one of the men called.

Jake ignored him, jumping up and down on the flexible limb. Finally, the men disregarded him. David watched the tree shudder and jump as the limbs hooked on brush and other vegetation.

Jake laughed loudly all the way down, even when he barely managed to hang on.

"Too bad yer such a baby," he told David when they reached the bottom. "You'd be havin' fun like me if you wasn't so scared all the time."

David swallowed a quick retort. He hadn't realized he'd been scared much at all on the entire journey.

Jake still always brought his blanket and slept beside David. One night David sat up. "Want to hear how much God loves you?" he asked.

Jake sat up too. "How much?"

"Enough to die for you, Jake."

"That don't even make sense, baby Davy. What's it

"ENOUGH TO DIE FOR YOU, JAKE"

supposed to mean?"

David thought a moment. "Well, let's say you rode the big tree down the hill and hurt someone. Penberry said you'd have to have a good lickin'. But I felt sorry for you and took your lickin' for you. Would you think I loved you a lot?"

Jake thought a moment then nodded. "Guess you'd have to."

"That's what happened, Jake. When God first created people, they just kept on living. They didn't die. God told Adam and Eve if they sinned they'd have to die. They sinned but Jesus felt so sorry for them, He died in their place."

Jake thought some more. "You sure about that, baby Davy? He really did that? Maybe I oughta figure this out. What should I do?"

"Simple. Just thank Him for dying for you and tell Him you love Him. If you don't really love Him, ask Him to help you love Him. Then ask Him to send His

"MAYBE I OUGHTA FIGURE THIS OUT"

Holy Spirit to love you and show you how to follow Him. That's it, Jake. Want to do it now?"

"Uh—don't get too pushy, baby Davy. I'll think about it."

The next days consisted of the oxen straining every muscle climbing a steep hill, then waiting for the men to bring the ox and tree.

Jake followed the huge ox and big tree, riding it down each time. "I make it heavier and that helps hold the wagons back," he told David. "But my feet're gettin' terrible sore. Think I could use yours?"

David shook his head. "You can try, but your feet are bigger than mine." Jake couldn't get David's shoes on.

"Thanks, baby Davy," Jake said. "I'm thinkin' about this God of yours who died so we wouldn't have to. You're kinda like Him, ain't you? Well, not that good, but you was goin' to give me your shoes."

David pretended to be asleep, but he thanked God

"DON'T GET TOO PUSHY, BABY DAVY"

silently for loving Jake so much.

One night when Jake dropped his blanket beside David's, he sat on it facing David. "Know what?" he asked. "Mules is smarter than oxen. Them oxen'll pull until they drop dead, but mules sure don't." He giggled, something David had never heard him do before. "When men start beatin' on the mules, they just fall down. So the oxen gotta pull all them wagons up these horble hills."

When they reached the top of the highest peak, the weary travelers rested a day to let the exhausted oxen recuperate.

"I can't walk no more on these sore feet," Jake told David.

Pa, building a fire nearby, heard. "I bet you could wear my shoes," he said. "I got some new ones in the wagon. Come try them." Jake tried and they fit well enough. He ran off with the shoes, looking happy. But he didn't thank Pa.

"I BET YOU COULD WEAR MY SHOES"

WAGONS WEST

Descending the Blue Mountains was easier, but still wearing on the people and animals as they climbed and descended hill after hill, each a little lower than the last. At last, they reached the valley below.

Suddenly, wagons and wagon trains were everywhere, in front of them, behind them, to the side. The Penberry train rested for two days with plenty of grass and water.

Indians roamed around the train. Sometimes, they tried to sell or swap things; sometimes they tried to communicate, sometimes they just passed.

Four Indian boys about David and Jake's age stopped and wanted to throw rocks at an old wagon wheel.

"I ain't that dumb," Jake said.

David laughed. "You remember getting beat throwing rocks, don't you? Come on, Jake. Let's play with them."

The Indians beat the white boys in the rock-throwing game. Then David taught them to play baseball.

DAVID TAUGHT THEM TO PLAY BASEBALL

Early in the afternoon, David's mother invited them all to eat soup and bread. David enjoyed the first real bread he'd had for months.

"Why don't we have a wrestling tournament?" Jake suggested later in the afternoon.

When the Indians understood what they wanted to do, the tournament began. David lost the first match, so he watched Jake beat every one of the Indians.

The Indian boys didn't mind. They showed Jake and David how to prick their fingers and share blood. They all became blood brothers that day.

Late that night an Indian chief, wearing a full feathered head-dress, strutted into camp with the four boys who'd played with David and Jake. Immediately, a group of white men surrounded them.

The Indian Chief made motions of wrestling, then he made them understand he wanted to see the white boy who could beat four Indians.

Jake stepped forward, his chest thrust out and

HE WANTED TO SEE THE WHITE BOY

proud look in his eyes. The chief felt Jake's arm muscles, and looked him over carefully, checking his thighs, chest, back and calves. Even his teeth.

Then he nodded and turned to the men around them. He made motions of putting something in his left hand with his right, then pointed at Jake. Suddenly, it hit David! The Chief wanted to buy Jake!

David couldn't help it. He broke out laughing.

"What's going on?" Pa asked. "What does he want?"

When David told him, Pa didn't laugh. "How do you tell an Indian Chief he can't have what he wants?" he asked, a worried look on his face.

The men finally made the Indian understand they couldn't sell their children.

The Indian didn't call a war party as the whites had feared. Instead, he motioned Jake to follow him. When Jake went, the Chief gave him a beautiful black and white pony.

PA DIDN'T LAUGH

"I AIN'T SELLING THAT PONY"

CHAPTER 12

David laughed again. "Now, you have something to sell and get some money."

"I ain't sellin' that pony. How many Indian Chiefs gave you somethin'?"

The time came to move on. Animals and humans all felt too tired to go. Two days later, they camped beside the John Day River, staying an extra day as the animals were unable to go on.

A day and a half later, they reached the mighty Columbia River at noon. David stood on the bank, looking across the wide river at the rounded sandy hills on the other side. Many Indians fished in the river and some brought salmon to trade.

The train hit the Deschutes River three miles away later in the afternoon and camped there.

The next morning, they headed for The Dalles where they'd decide how to get over the Cascade Mountains which were worse than The Blues. To go down the river, which was treacherous and expensive, they had to put everything on boats. The other choice, The Barlow Road, was so steep many animals died trying to climb it.

After discussing the costs and dangers, the train decided to take the Barlow Road.

They traveled for two days in beautiful wooded country with good grass for the animals. The men decided to rest three days before entering the mountains, hoping the animals would gain enough strength to make it.

Fires shone in the woods all around as others prepared for the grueling journey ahead.

Jake still threw his blanket down beside David's every night. "We're making history, Jake," David said one night when Jake arrived.

"Who cares?" Jake grunted. "I jist wanna git somewhere. Hey, I decided I don't care if Annie spends her

"WE'RE MAKING HISTORY, JAKE"

time with that ugly feller. You like me, don't you?

"Sure, I like you a lot. So does God."

"Good. Think she'd give my gold back?"

David smiled to himself in the dark. "She might. Why don't you ask her?"

"You gotta ask her."

"Sure. Tell me what to say."

"Just tell her to go ahead and ruin her life with that piece of junk."

When David gave Annie Jake's message, she laughed and got the stone for Jake. "Don't tell him, but Papa thinks it's not gold. I hope it is, though."

The next day, a grizzled old man stopped at the Moreland fire to talk. "Why you goin' this way anyhow?"

"Cause we've heard how fertile and free Oregon City is," Pa said. "It'll all be worth it when we get there."

The man shook his long white hair. "No, 'twon't,"

"WHY YOU GOIN' THIS WAY, ANYHOW?"

he said. "I jist come from Oregon City. Too much hustle and bustle fer me. It's so full of people, ain't hardly room for more. Most donation claims been taken, too. I seen a purty little valley northeast of here, the Walla Walla Valley, just now open to settlers. Been closed while they chased the Injuns out, but they're gone now.

"Me'n my fam'ly's goin' back to Walla Walla Valley and git us our donation claim and settle down."

Pa looked at Ma and Ma looked at Pa. "Should I go talk to the others?" he asked.

The wagon train stayed two more days talking to the man, to others, and among themselves.

Finally, the men decided to go back to the Walla Walla Valley and have a look. "We didn't come all this way to find a bustlin' city where ain't no more free land," one of the men said.

"'Sides," another said, "we'd lose a bunch of livestock sure, goin' over that mountain."

"WE DIDN'T COME ALL THIS WAY TO FIND A BUSTLIN' CITY"

The train didn't hurry back, taking time for the animals to eat all the grass they could find.

Evenings, the old man told stories around the camp fire. "Didja know some Injuns call The Oregon Trail, The Great Medicine Road of the White Man?" he said one night.

David found that interesting. "Why did they call it that?" he asked.

The man shook his grizzled white hair. "Don't rightly know. Prob'ly thought it was healthier in the west."

They decided to stop at the Columbia River and try to catch some enormous salmon like the Indians had. Jake joined David on a rock overhanging the river. "My fish'll be twicet as big as yers," he said.

As they fished in the warm sunshine, David grew sleepy. Almost dozing, he heard a big splash below. Suddenly wide awake, he looked around. Jake! Jake wasn't on the rock with him anymore! He raced down

JAKE WASN'T ON THE ROCK WITH HIM ANYMORE

to the river's edge to find Jake struggling in deep water downstream a few feet. David jerked off his boots, ran downstream twenty feet ahead of Jake and threw himself into the water.

He found Jake in the deep swirling water, and reached an arm around him, pulling his head above water. Jake jerked away and dropped back under. David grappled for Jake's long hair and jerked him to the top again. Jake grabbed David's arms and tried to hang on. David went under with Jake. Terrified, David gave Jake's arms two mighty whacks and surfaced. "Help me, God," he yelled, gulping in two quick breaths. "I can't do this without You." Diving again, he found Jake. This time, Jake didn't resist so David pulled him to shore, dragged him out of the water, turned him on his stomach, and began pushing the water from him.

When Jake stopped coughing, he jerked his knees under him, knocking David off. "What ya tryin' to do,

"HELP ME, GOD... I CAN'T DO THIS WITHOUT YOU"

break my back?" he growled.

"Not that you'd care," David yelled, "but I'm trying to save your life."

By that time, several people arrived to tend to Jake, so David ran back to the rock and got their fishing poles.

That night when Jake threw down his blanket beside David's, he sat on it, facing David. "You didn't hafta hold my arms down so tight. Din't ya know it hurt me?"

"When did I hold your arms down?"

"Davy! When you drug me outta the river. How'd ya do it anyway? Holdin' both my arms tight and swimmin' to the shore draggin' me?"

"I didn't hold your arms at all, Jake. I just held you and swam as hard as I could. You kept grabbing me, you know."

"But at the last you held my arms against my sides. Tight. I couldn't move nothin'. Your fingers dug right into my hide."

"HOW'D YA DO IT ANYWAY?"

Suddenly, David knew what happened. "An angel held you, Jake. An angel saved your life today. You'd better be thanking God for it, too."

Jake looked confused. Finally, he nodded. "You might be right. You'd a'needed four arms to do all that, wouldn't you?" He leaned over and peered into David's eyes. "Did you ask your God to help?"

David nodded. "I sure did. I was in bad trouble. He saved both our lives, Jake. Should we thank Him now?"

Jake hesitated a moment. "Uh—go ahead, if you want."

David bowed his head and closed his eyes. "Dear Heavenly Father. Thank You for loving each one of us as if we were your only child. Thank You for loving us so much You gave Your only Son to die for us so we can live with You forever. Thank You for always watching over us and especially for saving our lives today. Forgive our sins and send Your Holy Spirit to

"THANK YOU FOR LOVING US SO MUCH YOU GAVE YOUR ONLY SON"

draw us closer to You each day. Thank You again. We love You, Father and we pray in Jesus' name. Amen.

Jake closed his eyes. "Yeah. Thanks fer savin' our lives." He looked at David a moment and nodded. "Guess I oughta thank you, too, baby Davy." He thought a moment. "Maybe you ain't no baby, Dave. You did good today."

Two weeks later, on September 18, the train crested a small hill. "There it is!" the old man said, waving his arm over the scene ahead. "There's Walla Walla Valley. Ain't it somethin'?"

David nodded. Trees bordered the several small rivers running through the peaceful little valley. Dry grass covered the low rolling hills. It looked pleasant.

David felt excited. Could the journey really be over? It seemed they'd been traveling forever. His eyes fell on the stumbling oxen. Surely, they could make it now. The valiant animals deserved a long rest.

Late in the afternoon, David stopped Thunder at the

"THERE IT IS!"

west end of what must be a short street. Dismounting, he looked around. Some tepees stood north of the street which looked like a trail, with four rickety buildings on each side. A few buildings speckled the landscape south, then the land went on and on.

The old man appeared beside David. "This here's a Nez Perce Indian trail," he said. "The land hain't been ruined yet, and donations' claims kin be taken anywhere's around. See them trees past the buildin's? That's a creek. Mill Creek it's called."

Pa appeared and dropped a big hand over David's shoulder. "Think we could make a home here? It'll be hard work—and you and I'll have to do most of it, but it looks good to me."

David looked across the valley again. It looked good to him, too. Pa took off his hat and looked up. "Thank You, God, for bein' with us on our long, hard journey. Thank You for bein' with us here as we build a home and community. Help us to always remember, no

"THINK WE COULD MAKE A HOME HERE?"

matter what we try, we can't do it without You. But with You, nothing's impossible. Thank You again and again. In Jesus' name. Amen."

David nodded. "Yes, Lord," he added. "With You we can do anything—and everything—in this wonderful, new land. And we will, too."

"YES, LORD... WITH YOU, WE CAN DO ANYTHING"

AWESOME BOOKS FOR KIDS!

The Young Reader's Christian Library
Action, Adventure, and Fun Reading!

This series for young readers ages 8 to 12 is action-packed, fast-paced, and Christ-centered! With exciting illustrations on every other page following the text, kids won't be able to put these books down! Over 100 illustrations per book. All books are paperbound. The unique size (4 3/16" x 5 3/8") makes these books easy to take anywhere!

A Great Selection to Satisfy All Kids!

Abraham Lincoln	In His Steps	Prudence of Plymouth
Ben-Hur	Jesus	Plantation
Billy Sunday	Joseph	Robinson Crusoe
Christopher Columbus	Lydia	Roger Williams
Corrie ten Boom	Miriam	Ruth
David Livingstone	Paul	Samuel Morris
Deborah	Peter	The Swiss Family
Elijah	The Pilgrim's Progress	Robinson
Esther	Pocahontas	Taming the Land
Heidi	Pollyanna	Thunder in the Valley
Hudson Taylor		Wagons West

Available wherever books are sold.

Or order from: Barbour Publishing, Inc., P.O. Box 719
Uhrichsville, Ohio 44683
http://www.barbourbooks.com

$2.50 each retail, plus $1.00 for postage and handling per order. Prices subject to change without notic